DIA

NINJA

SPY

3

Where evil goes, the ninja will follow...

Also by William Thomas and Peter Patrick:

Diary of a Ninja Spy

Diary of a Ninja Spy 2

Diary of a Ninja Spy 4

Diary of a Ninja Spy 5

In the 'Diary of a Super Spy' series:

Diary of a Super Spy

Diary of a Super Spy 2: Attack of the Ninjas!

Diary of a Super Spy 3: A Giant Problem!

Diary of a Super Spy 4: Space!

Diary of a Super Spy 5: Evil Attack!

Diary of a Super Spy 6: Daylight Robbery!

Diary of a Ninja Spy 3
(Ninja Ghost Attack!)

William Thomas
Peter Patrick

Chapter 1

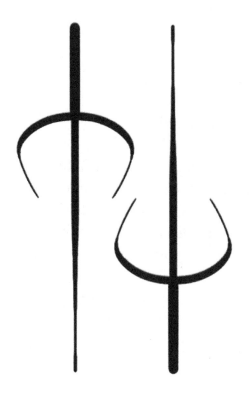

"If there are sixty minutes in one hour, and there are twenty dogs in the car, how long does it take an owl to fly around the school and eat a lollipop?"

OMG!

This is *sooo* boring!

I'm a **NINJA SPY!**

I don't need to know any of this nonsense. But here I am – a super-secret Ninja Spy - stuck in this boring math class at school. I should be fighting bad guys, but the Ninja Spy Agency believes it is important I still lead a 'normal' life.

I lean across my table to Emily, the cutest girl in school, and try to impress her with my recruitment into the elite Ninja Spy Agency.

"Blake," Emily whispers to me, trying not to get the attention of our teacher, "I was there when you meet them. It is not a secret to me. Frankly, I'm getting a little tired of hearing about your wild adventures."

Wait! What?

Tired of my amazing feats?

She must be jealous. I lean across my table to the other side where Fred, my best friend, is sitting.

"Do you want to hear more of my secret adventures, Fred?"

"Not now Blake," Fred says under his breath, "I want to learn math!"

"Sigh," I say, rolling my eyes, "Make it stop, it is so boring."

Instantly my teacher turns around and glares at me, "Blake, if I hear your voice again during my class, I will cover you in honey and lock you up in a box full of ants!"

BTW, my math teacher is tough. Probably borderline crazy.

Last week, she took little Jeremy Wilson and hung him upside down from the school flag pole. She left him there until he learnt all his times-tables. It took him three days...

But her methods work, and I sink into my seat, trying to focus. Luckily, the rest of the lesson goes quickly and soon I am having lunch with Emily and Fred.

Ever since my recruitment into the Ninja Spy Agency, I've become fairly confident around the school yard. This confidence has not gone unnoticed and I have attracted unwanted attention from one of the alpha bullies on campus.

His name is Bull.

Yes, Bull the Bully.

That's his actual name too - Bull the Bully Benjamin Bowen. Some parents come up with the dumbest names.

"Hey, twerp."

I continue to walk across the courtyard with Emily and Fred.

"Hey! I'm talking to you, twerp."

I'm going to just keep walking - but then I feel a sudden jolt.

I've been lifted in the air!

"I hear you are a tough guy now?" states Bull.

"No, no, no, I'm not. Not me, ah uh, no way," I reply.

I must keep my Ninja abilities a secret.

As a secret Ninja Spy, I cannot let anyone know about my abilities.

Even though I want to do a triple-fly, super-jump kick on Bull, I cannot use my abilities at school.

When I don't fight back, Bull walks me across to the basketball hoop and shoots. I swish through the hoop and become tangled in the net!

Emily and Fred are staring at me.

This is so embarrassing, especially after I was telling them how cool I've become now that I'm a Ninja Spy.

Damn.

I must look ridiculous.

It won't be today, but I'll get my sweet revenge on you, Bull.

****

After school, I don't wait for my friends, instead I leave in a hurry for the Ninja Spy Agency headquarters. I didn't want to see them much anyway - I still feel ashamed of the bully incident.

I wish I could use my Ninja abilities at school. That would be so cool.

I go through the series of password and identification checks in order to enter the headquarters. Fingerprint scanner, pupil scan, secret questions and a 307-digit password. Security is *really* tight here.

I walk into the strategy room to find Tekato, my mentor, pacing back and forth. He is clearly worried about something.

"Whew, what a day at school!" I say to him, trying to take his mind off his troubles.

"We had math class and I got a special mention from the teacher for being the smartest there." A little white lie, but I must have the Ninja Spy Agency believe I'm very intelligent as well as incredibly tough.

"No one is interested in your day at school, Blake," Tekato responses. "We have a bigger problem. Some of our rare and valuable artifacts are being stolen from our vaults around the world. These items of worth are kept in top secret locations under heavy guard. No one should ever be able to break in and steal from us."

"Ohhh," I say. I would much rather be on an important mission than do my stupid Ninja Spy training homework. "So what exactly has been stolen?"

"I shouldn't tell you, as you are still only a newbie here. But in times like this, maybe it is good to have input from someone as uneducated and inexperienced as you."

Uneducated and inexperienced?!

Well, that hurts a bit. I've been here 3 weeks and saved the day twice already!

"Very old, fragile and powerful books are being stolen. To be more exact – the ancient Spell books!" concludes Tekato.

"Spell books?! Like magic and stuff?"

"Yes Blake, like magic and stuff."

"Can you teach me that stuff too?" I ask.

"At the Ninja Spy Agency, we don't use magic spells because they are very hard to learn and control. These spell books are useless to most people because they are written in a secret ninja language. Many of us here, in the modern world, have never seen the spells in action," Tekato explains as he starts to fidget more and more. He certainly is worried about this. "Blake, do you want to go and have a look at one of our secret vault locations? Maybe you can see something that our highly trained elite personal cannot," Tekato asks, reinforcing the idea that I'm not highly trained.

"I'll do it!" I scream. This will be a great chance to rekindle my friend's faith in my abilities.

"Blake, one more thing before you go. Stored at the location is one of our super-rare spell books - The Chronicles of Ninja Spells Book 11, Volume 11, Issue 984."

Wow, that's a title. How many spell books are there?

"Remember someone is after them and there is a chance you may not be safe. In fact, you may never come back," adds Tekato.

"Oh," I whisper.

Hmmm, I feel like he should have told me about the dangers before I said I'd go. Especially if I'm not 'highly trained'.

He shakes my hand as if I'll never see him again.

"Good luck," he finishes.

Tekato then whispers something, "Murr-murr-murr-murr."

"Sorry, I couldn't hear you."

"Murr-murr-murr-murr," he mumbles again under his breath. Tekato is leading me towards the front door.

"What are you trying to say?" I question.

"Thereisprobablyaninjaghostthere,byebye," blurts out Tekato.

What did he say? I replay his words slowly in my head… *there is probably a ninja ghost there.*

What!? Panic!!

Ninja Ghost!!

Chapter 2

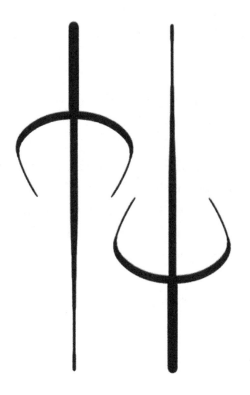

I arrive on a remote island with Emily and Fred via a six-hour helicopter ride.

I have brought my two friends along to witness my dangerous adventures. I need to rebuild my tough-cool guy image after the incident with Bull.

The helicopter pilot drops us off on the beach and flies away.

Pulling out the map that Tekato gave me, we start marching in the direction of the secret vault. For the next few hours we cut our way through the thick tropical jungle trying to get to the massive rock formation.

"Up there on top of this rock is the vault," I say.

"Whew, I didn't realize that this was going to be such hard work," gasps Fred.

"My friend, being an elite Ninja Spy is only for the fittest," I gloat.

"Blake, it really wasn't necessary that you bring us here to prove you're a super ninja," says Emily, "In fact, I'm more disappointed in you now. You should know you don't need to prove yourself to us - we are your friends."

"In that case, there is something else I should tell you, Emily."

"What's that?"

"I wasn't meant to bring you here. Tekato gave me strict orders not to take anyone else on this mission, but I brought you two along to see the cool stuff I do in the Ninja Spy Agency," I reply.

They aren't going to be happy about this.

"What!? So you brought us along to simply prove you are cool?" cuts in Fred, "We're not meant to be here?!"

"Yeah, sorry."

"Why did Tekato tell you not to bring anyone?" questions Emily.

I stare at the ground and grumble, "'Cos it could get sort of dangerous…"

"BLAKE!" screams Emily. She is not happy.

"Why is it dangerous, Blake?" Emily moves closer to me with her hands on her hips. I can see the fury in her flaring nostrils.

"There might be a small, minute, microscopic, tiny chance that we may encounter a… ninja ghost …."

"BLAKE!" Emily screams even louder this time.

She is really, really mad.

I turn to look at Fred to see if he is excited about the idea of a ninja ghost.

Nope.

He has fainted.

"Get me off this island now, Blake!" demands Emily, "NOW!"

"Uh, my bad again. The only way to contact Headquarters is through a secure phone line located in the vault at the top of this rock," I say apologetically.

Fred starts to wake up and he is really pale.

"You OK, Fred?" I ask.

"Me? No, I am not OK! I hate ghosts."

I should have known he hated ghosts, he is scared of everything. And when I say everything, I mean everything. Yesterday, he wouldn't sit down in class because he was scared of the chair. The chair!

But I can tell he is really scared now because he is shaking uncontrollably.

"We are here now," I say dismissing any anger towards me, "Let's make the most of it."

A little positive attitude can go a long way.

"Blake," says Emily with no emotion.

"Yes, my partner in adventure?"

"Get. Me. Off. This. Island."

Ekkk, I think I'm more scared of Emily than any ninja ghost!

"To the top then!" I smile nervously and run towards the base of the rock.

At the top, I look around and there is a cave entrance. We walk in together once the others finally catch up to me at the top. Inside the cave, we find a large medieval-looking door.

"There is nobody else here," I say surprised. "There are meant to be elite ninja spies guarding this location. Where are there?"

"Blake. Look the vault door is ajar," Fred points out.

"Do you think someone is in there?" asks Emily.

"Ha, not a chance. They would have heard us coming and run away," I explain. "The two of you go in and see for yourself, I'll stay guard out here."

"Noooo, if you are so sure no one is in there, you should go in first!" explodes Emily.

"Fine."

I pry open the door to get in and turn on my Ninja Spy flashlight. The vault is the size of a standard bedroom with a display case in the middle of the room.

There is a book in the display case - it must be the Ninja Spell book! We have found it and it's safe. I turn and invite the others into the vault.

"Look guys, it is completely safe, and the Spell Book is still safe too!"

"Blake?" asks Fred.

"Is this one of your pathetic jokes?"

"What do you mean? None of my jokes are pathetic jokes. Listen, here's a good joke – You know, I stayed up all last night wondering where the sun went… and then it dawned on me! Ha!"

"Uh, guys," Emily interrupts us, pointing at the display case. "Look."

An empty display case!

The Spell Book is gone.

Someone has stolen it!

And they were quick!

It was only out of my vision for 10 seconds…

Chapter 3

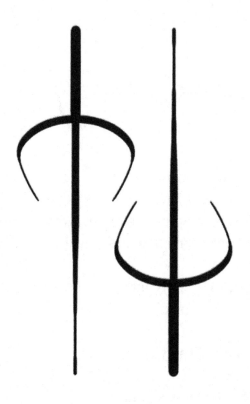

"Where is it? I thought it was just here!"

Suddenly a soft glowing light emits from the far corner of the room. Then it becomes clear the light is holding the book!

A few seconds pass and the light transforms into… A GHOST!

"Argghhhh!" Emily, Fred and I scream together.

"Silence," speaks the ghost. "What are you children doing here?"

"We are here to protect the book you are holding! You are not going anywhere Ninja Ghost!" I yell out.

"Haw haw, you cannot stop me. The ninja guards that were here have ran off in fear. I suggest you do the same," shouts the Ninja Ghost.

"OK, we are outta here," says Emily, slowly shuffling towards the door.

I turn to see what Fred is doing, and he is on the ground sleeping. Oh, actually he's not sleeping - he must have fainted again.

"I won't let you leave this room!" I yell out.

I charge to the door and race past Emily, who is trying to get out. Once I'm on the outside of the vault, I slam it shut and quickly lock it with the padlock.

"Blake!" I hear Emily scream from inside the vault.

Whoops.

Major whoops!

I feel as if I just made a pretty large mistake.

I have locked my friends in a vault with a dangerous ninja ghost!

To make it worse, I don't have the padlock key.

"Sorry! I am so sorry! I'll just find the key!" I yell out.

I don't know what the key looks like or where it could be!

This is totally bad - I really hope the ninja ghost doesn't harm them!

"Oh dear, you are in big trouble," says a voice behind me.

It's the **Ninja Ghost!**

"How did you get out here?!" I ask.

"I'm a ghost. I can walk through walls," he puts his hand through the wall to demonstrate. "Dude, you should spend more time in school learning the simple stuff."

"I won't let you go!" I yell at him.

"Little ninja boy, I am unstoppable. I can walk through almost anything and can turn invisible at any time I want."

He vanishes in front of me, but I can still hear his voice.
Then he quickly reappears.

I throw a left foot kick at him. It seemed like a rocking kick - it should have knocked him flat!

But he is still standing!

"Haha, you cannot touch me, I am a ghost! Only I can control if you can touch me or not."

"That's unfair," I say to him. "How am I meant to fight you?"

"Ha ha! You cannot fight me - but I can fight you! You will be no challenge for me at all," replies the Ninja Ghost.

Eeekk.

This is so not good.

"Don't fear, I am not going to harm you or your friends. They are really mad at you, anyway. I'd rather see them get their vengeance on you. It will be more satisfying," laughs the ghost holding the Spell Book.

I make a dive at the Spell Book! I want it back!

I get a hand on it, but then the Ninja Ghost yanks it away!

As it pulls the book away, I manage to tear a page from the book.

"Do you think you can simply reach out and take my loot from me? Haw Haw!" he laughs.

The ghost continues his stupid laugh as he floats his way down the rock formation with the book.

Why do all the bad guys have such stupid laughs?

"Don't worry guys, the Ninja Ghost is gone. I frightened him off," I lie to help calm my friends, who are still locked in the vault.

"Blake! You better get us out of here ASAP!" Emily seems really unhappy.

"I'm on it!" I yell as I tie on my Ninja Spy mask.

Action time!

Chapter 4

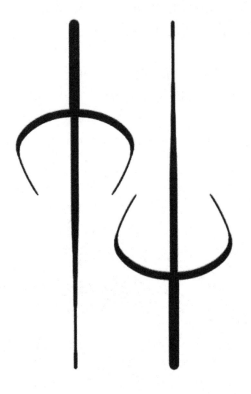

Oh man, I'm so dead once Tekato finds out that I brought my friends on this recon mission.

He is going to be mad - in fact, he will probably kick me out of the Ninja Spy Agency.

I either need to find the key to the vault or find a way of breaking Emily and Fred out of there. I could chase after the Ninja Ghost but he is a long way from me now and I'll never catch him. He probably didn't use a key anyway.

"Blake, are you there?" Emily yells through the vault door.

"Yeah, I'm still here."

"Fred is still out cold, he must have gotten a genuine fright by the ghost. There is a phone in here, should I call for help?" asks Emily.

"No, don't! That is a secure line back to headquarters. If they find out you're in there, I'll be in a lot of trouble. It has to be me who calls HQ. You two weren't meant to be here," I reply.

"That is not my problem, Blake! They will have the key to the door! You have 5 minutes to get us out, then I'm calling them. Understood?" states Emily.

"OK then."

Wow, she can be mean. I better start working out how I'm going to get them out without the vault key. Think, Blake, think!

I know!

I'll go in through the top of the rock with help from my pocket rocket!

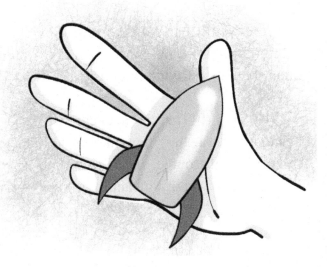

The pocket rocket is a little missile the size of my hand, but it is a very powerful spy gadget!

It can easily take me to space, however today I need it to do a different task - take the top off a rock face!

I attach a heap of vines to the back of the rocket and rapidly tie them around the rocks.

Now - time to hit the ignition…

The rocket takes off!

And then… **CRACK!**

The pocket rocket worked! It has ripped the top off the rock!

"Hey, did you see that?!" I yell into the top of the vault.

"Hmmff," Emily says, not impressed at all.

"I got you out!" I restate my achievement.

No response.

"It's me, Blake!" I say in case they can't recognize me when I'm wearing my ninja mask.

"I know it is you! You put us in here!" Emily snaps back. "Help me carry Fred out of here."

"Wow, he has been out a long time. Do you think he is OK?" I ask.

"Obviously he is not OK, you moron. You have scared him half to death! Now, we have to carry him home!"

"I'll make the call from the secure line and then we need to get back to the beach for pick up. More importantly, I need to find a way to defeat the Ninja Ghost!"

Chapter 5

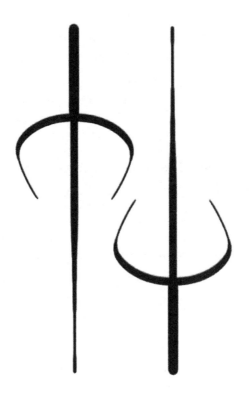

"Tekato!" I yell. "I came face to see-through face with the Ninja Ghost!"

"Blake! Good to see you. I was worried that you didn't make it. You're very lucky you survived an encounter with the Ninja Ghost! The Ninja Spies we had guarding the vault told me they ran off as soon as they thought the Ninja Ghost was in the vault with the Spell Book," says Tekato. "How did you survive?"

"He thought I was in greater danger from… um… another threat, and he let me be."

"You are very lucky, Blake. Most people who have encountered the Ninja Ghost have ended up in terrible pain. If only you had someone else there to verify your story, because some agents here won't believe you."

"Urrrr, I may have a few witnesses…" I say cautiously.

Tekato gives me a stern look.

"He he," I joke, "the Ninja Ghost was my witness."

"Blake, while you were gone on your mission, we have concluded that the Ninja Ghost is stealing our Spell Books for a specific reason," explains Tekato as he paces around the room.

Turning around, I realize that everyone in HQ is rushing. Something has really moved the agency into panic mode.

"Why would he steal your Spell Books?" I ask Tekato.

Tekato stops pacing.

"The Ninja Ghost is trying to build a ghost army of ninjas!" he says with a trembling voice.

"Whoa, cool!" I react.

"No, not cool, Blake!" rebuts Tekato. "If he succeeds, we will never stop them. He will rule the world, which is a problem because he is a really, really nasty ghost."

"Then we need to stop him!" I yell.

"That will be hard, if not impossible."

"Hmmmm," I say, trying to join in on the drama. I'm just acting here - I wouldn't even know where to start defeating the Ninja Ghost. As I pace back and forth with Tekato, I feel the page I ripped from the Spell Book in my pocket.

"Hey Tekato, would this help?" I smooth the page and show Tekato.

"Oh boy!" I hear a voice from the doorway. It's the ninja guru, the Grandmaster…

"Where did you get that?" he demands.

"I was trying to save your Spell Book from the Ninja Ghost, but this is all I got," I say.

The tiny fragile old man moves towards me and looks at the page.

I had a look at the page earlier and it was all in gibberish, just scribbles and symbols. The Grandmaster seems to be reading it.

"Are you reading this messy garbage," I ask.

The worried look on the Grandmaster's face turns from horror to optimism.

"We may have a way of defeating the Ninja Ghost!" he yells with hope. "This page says that you can only defeat a ninja ghost with another ninja ghost."

"Yo, Mr. Grandmaster," I say respectably, "We don't have another ninja ghost."

"But we can!"

Uh oh, I don't like the way he is staring at me.

"The page you are holding contains a spell to turn someone into a ghost," he pauses, then laughs, "Little man, you will become a *ghost!*"

Chapter 6

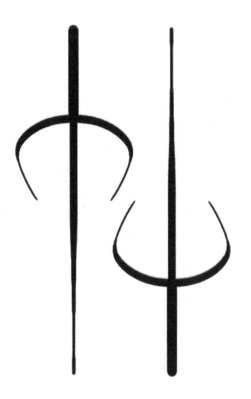

In a rush, the Grandmaster leads me to the secrecy floor above the basement (which is not really a secret floor because everyone knows it exists).

"Now stand there," directs the Grandmaster while pointing to the middle of the floor.

"Nobody has asked me if I want to become a ghost," I announce.

"Shhh boy," the Grandmaster completely disregards my feelings about transforming into a spirit. "I haven't used this spell before, hopefully I can get it right on the first try."

"Ahhhhh... what do you mean, get it right on the first try? What happens if you fail? Is this going to hurt?!"

"It may not hurt, or it may hurt a little," he pauses, "Or it may hurt a lot."

Before I get an opportunity to voice my concerns, the Grandmaster starts chanting out the spell written on the ripped page.

"Uba- uba- uba- duba-duba," he repeats over and over.

And to make this more ridiculous, he is also dancing.

It's a strange dance, as if he is channeling his inner dolphin.

I'm pretty sure whatever he is saying is not going to work...

Pop!

What on earth?

Something is different.

Am I a ghost?

I watch the Grandmaster looking confused and scratching his head. I look down at my body.

Aw man!

I'm not a ghost!

I am a **giant grub!**

"No, no, that doesn't look right," stammers the old Grandmaster. "Uza- uza- uza- zuba-zuba!"

Oh great, now he is doing an even more stupid dance.

BAM!

"Hmmm," the Grandmaster lets out.

I look down at my body again. **What!?** Now I am a giant sock!?

PEEF!

He tries again.

Wrong again!

Now I'm a tiny tree!

PLATT!

Arr, now a toilet!

DOOF!

A Sausage!

CRACK!

Donut.

FIZZ!

A massive wrestler. Cool!

"Hey, leave me like this…"

ZIPPO!

"A-ha! There, I have done it! You are now a ghost!"

I look down at my body and he is right, I'm a ghost!

"Ooooooohhhhhhhh," I moan, "I aaaammmm aaa gggghhhossstttt."

"You don't need to talk like that," states the Grandmaster.

"Oookkkkkk," I groan. I can't help myself.

Now that I am a ghost, I can do ghost things!

My first task is to walk through a wall.

"See ya' later!" I yell to the Grandmaster as I walk straight through the wall to the next room.

Wow, that is cool.

The problem is I have just walked into the girl's locker room.

"Argh, ghost!" one girl screams.

Ekk!

I need to get back to the Grandmaster!

I dart back through the wall.

"Ho ho! You didn't get far, did you, boy?" laughs the Grandmaster.

"Now try and be invisible," he commands.

PING!

I think about turning invisible and then… I turn invisible!

"Very good," states the Grandmaster. "You will need to carry this with you."

"What is it?"

"It is a ghost prison."

He shows me a box the size of a door, but then he folds it up so it can fit into my pocket.

"You are ready to fight the Ninja Ghost."

"Soon!" I blurt out. While I'm a ghost, I have a few things to sort out first.

"Don't get distracted! You must stay on task! You only have a certain amount of time before the spell becomes permanent!"

"How much time do I have?"

"Exactly 10 hours!"

"Heaps of time, I'll be back soon!"

I'm going to have some fun with this…

Chapter 7

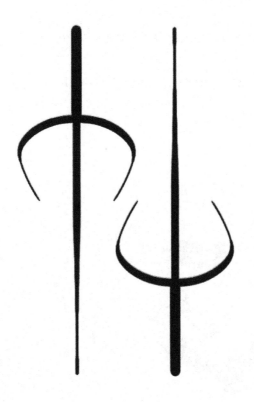

There is a bully that I need to deal a dose of vengeance too. Watch out Bull the Bully - here comes Blake the Ghost Ninja Spy!

As I get close to Bull's favorite hangout, the park, a stray dog comes up to me and wants to play.

"Shoo," I whisper. "How can you see me? I am invisible!"

The stray dog keeps harassing me.

It must be able to see me! The dog must have a rare ability to see ghosts! And the stray dog is super friendly too.

I could stay and play but I don't have a lot of time. I only have 10 hours to harass Bull, defeat the Ninja Ghost and get back to the Grandmaster.

But the dog is so cute…Oh, all right then, just for a few minutes.

A few hours later, the cute dog is finally getting tired and lies down for a nap. Good – now it is time for me to get back to pranking Bull.

I see him across the park throwing around small children for fun.

Sneaking up on Bull, I whisper in his ear, "Bull, you are stupid."

"Hey! Who said that!?" he yells out.

The small children all look at him, laugh and then run away. As they run away, I can hear them say that crazy Bull is losing his marbles.

"Who is there?" continues Bull.

"It is I, your future self, talking to you, Bull," I whisper.

"My future self?" Bull reacts. "That's impossible!"

"No, it is possible. I'm your future self and I've come back in time to warn you."

"Warn me of what?" Bull is beginning to believe that I am him from the future.

"I am here to warn you of the consequences of your actions," I say. And just for an added effect, I start to flick his ears.

Oh man, being a ghost is great fun!

"You must respect Blake. He is very powerful in the future," I say.

"Who? Who is Blake?"

What? He doesn't even know my name?

"Blake is the boy you pick on, you call him 'twerp'."

"Oh, twerp? Ha, twerp is never going to be powerful, you must have the wrong boy," says Bull.

"No, it is definitely twerp!" I say, realizing I have just called myself twerp.

"No way."

"Yes way! Leave Blake alone! In fact, every time you see him, you should bow."

"Haha! I'm not going to bow to that twerp."

I flick him hard across the ears.

"Trust me, I am you from the future. It is very bad for you to continue to harm Blake," I need a reason for him to fear his future, "Err... in the future, you are a belly dancer at Little Mac's big cheese burger franchise! Worse of all, Blake owns the store and you work for Blake!"

A look of horror spreads across his face. My prank has worked. I float off laughing! He will be no trouble at all from now on.

Right. Time to defeat the Ninja Ghost!

But…as I float away, I see a music store…
with drums! The Ninja Ghost will have to wait!

I know that Ninja Spies are meant to be
stealthy and silent, but I have other plans. I sit in
the shop and play the drums!

Cool!

As I am playing, I see the stray dog come up to
the shop window wagging its tail. Then I see the
Grandmaster. Ekkk!

"Boy! I know it's you in there," he screams
through the window. "Ninjas Spies do not drum!
You are meant to maintain a low profile!"

Oh, alright then.

"Time is ticking Blake! Remember - you only had 10 hours to complete your mission, and you have already wasted most of them!"

The Grandmaster is not much fun.

"Fine," I reluctantly agree. "Where should I go to find him?"

"I am not sure, but you need to look."

Then it occurs to me, "I know where!"

"Where?"

"A **ghost town!**"

Chapter 8

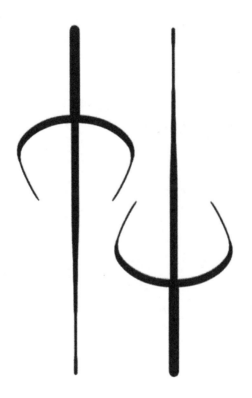

Luckily, the abandoned old ghost town isn't too far from where I live.

No one is sure why it was abandoned - some say it was because of poisoning, some say it was because it smelt funny and some say it was because of haunted spirits.

Whatever the case, it certainly deserves its name - the Ghost Town.

This place is my best chance of finding the Ninja Ghost.

The Ninja Ghost living in a ghost town sounds like a joke, but I am not laughing.

Actually, I'm terrified!

Which is strange again because I'm also a ghost!

Being a ghost is my only chance of defeating the Ninja Ghost.

But where is he?

Walking straight up the main road of the town, I cannot see another soul in sight.

"Hey Ninja Ghost!" I yell out. My voice echoes through the streets. "Want to fight me?"

No answer.

"Hey Ninja Ghost!" I try again.

Still nothing.

"Come on out and fight me! Are you scared?"

A second later, there is an answer…

"I'm not scared! I'm busy trying to create a ghost army! Go away!"

"I know why you are a ghost – it's because you have no guts!" Ha ha! What a great pun. "You're a gutless Ninja Ghost!"

Smash!

The Ninja Ghost pulls a great move and I am caught by surprise!

I'm thrown across the street!

"How did you become a ghost?" demands the Ninja Ghost.

"I had a spell put on me so I can stop you creating an army of ghost ninjas!"

"So… it is a fight you want? Just because you are now a ghost doesn't mean you can beat me! You think you can stop me? It's time to fight. But let's be quick, I have a lot of Spell Books to read!"

The Ninja Ghost throws a solid right hand punch but I float up into the air to avoid being hit. The floating thing is really cool! His second move, a left foot round-house kick, lands right in my chest.

Ouch. I go flying in the air and straight through a shop window!

But nothing breaks!

That's another advantage of being a ghost - no destruction. The one disadvantage is the Ninja Ghost can fully hit me.

I run back into the street for my ghost versus ghost fight!

I start bouncing around like a wild spring, ready to attack. The Ninja Ghost doesn't like it at all.

"Stay still!"

I strike a left hook to his lower back and follow it up with a short right jab.

But he shows me a move that I have never seen before.

It is so quick I don't even see what he did!

I go flying into another shop front.

Feeling dazed, I don't think I can keep fighting him like this.

I take the ghost prison out of my pocket, unfold it and put it to the side of me.

I bend forward and stick my head out of the wall, leaning into the street.

"Hey! Stupid ghost! Come and get me!"

He starts to move towards me. I pull my head back through the wall and move the ghost prison into position.

It works! He completely falls for my trap! He floats through the wall, straight into the prison. He is caught!

"Hey! Get me out of here!"

Not a chance! You are going to Ninja court!"

Chapter 9

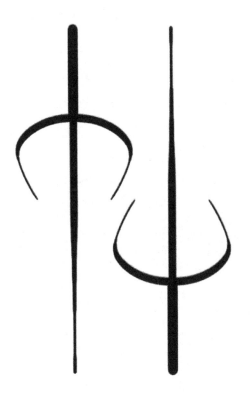

With the Ninja Ghost inside, I fold up the ghost prison, put it in my pocket and transport him back to HQ! Awesome.

"Where have you been!?" the Grandmaster yells.

"I've caught the Ninja Ghost!" I reply. I should totally get heaps of praise now.

"When you told me you did well in math class, were you lying?" asks Tekato, standing beside the Grandmaster.

"Ahhh, maybe I did not do as well as I made out... but that stuff's not important. I've got the Ninja Ghost!"

"Blake, you had 10 hours as a ghost, but then you needed to return here so I could transform you back to a person," the Grandmaster cuts in.

"Yeah, so?"

"You have been a ghost for 11 hours."

Wait! What? I do the math in my head.

Exploring as a ghost, 1 hour.
Played with the dog, 3 hours.
Played the drums, 2 hours.
Prank on Bull, 1 hour.
Travelled to the ghost town, 2 hours.
Fought the Ninja Ghost for 2 hours...

Ekk! Maybe I should pay attention in math class!

Chapter 10

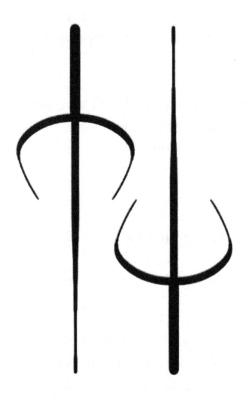

"Um, I don't want to stay as a ghost!" I complain. My Mom will kill me!

"You knew you only had 10 hours and yet you travelled around wasting time playing the drums and playing pranks as a ghost. Now you must stay as a ghost forever. I cannot change you back. I could only change you back to a person within 10 hours from the beginning of the spell."

"I'll call someone else to help," I say desperately.

"Who you gonna call?" says the Grandmaster.

"I don't know," I slump down on the ground and try to lean on the wall, but I fall through it.

"There is one person who can change you back. But I don't like your chances," adds the Grandmaster.

"Who!?" I jump up.

"The Ninja Ghost."

Urrr.

I slump back down. He isn't going to help me after I locked him up in a ghost prison.

"Only a ghost can undo a ghost after 10 hours."

"How about if we set him free as a trade?"

"No."

Really? Not even a second to think about it!

"You'll be fine," says Tekato, after standing silent for some time, "At least you won't be as lonely as he is in the ghost prison."

"Lonely! That's it!" I jump up and race out of the headquarters.

A few minutes later, I return with my bribe and go to the cell block where the Ninja Ghost is serving his time.

"Helllllooooo," I say cheerfully.

I probably shouldn't act so happy.

"What do you want?" snaps the Ninja Ghost.

"I need you to turn me back to a human," I answer.

"Ha ha ha," he laughs. "You took more than your 10 hours! Ha ha! No, you need to live with your mistake forever!"

"Well, I have something for you if you decide to help me. I know it will get pretty lonely being stuck in a ghost prison."

"Go on…"

"I present to you - a dog!"

"A dog?"

"A dog!"

"But dogs can't see me."

"This dog can!"

It is a huge success!

The Ninja Ghost puts on a wide smile. Lucky for me, he isn't a cat person.

"You can keep your new best friend if I walk out of here a human. Do we have a deal?"

"Deal," the Ninja Ghost smiles.

I guess everyone needs a friend.

Epilogue

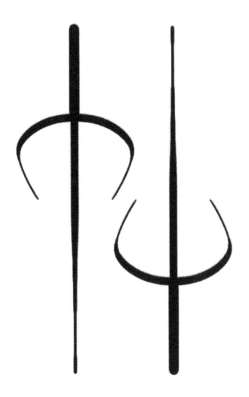

The following day on the way to school, I retell my Ninja Spy adventure to Emily and Fred.

They finally forgave me for taking them to a dangerous, remote island... but only after I agreed to do *all* their homework for the next month.

As we walk, I see Bull in the distance.

Oh no.

He gets up and walks towards our group.

He looks bigger than usual. He must have grown again.

Fred braces himself for an onslaught by Bull the Bully.

But Bull stops and bows to me.

I smirk, keep walking and give Emily and Fred a wink.

I can't wait for my next adventure…

The End

Also by William Thomas and Peter Patrick:

Diary of a Ninja Spy

Diary of a Ninja Spy 2

Diary of a Ninja Spy 4

Diary of a Ninja Spy 5

In the 'Diary of a Super Spy' series:

Diary of a Super Spy

Diary of a Super Spy 2: Attack of the Ninjas!

Diary of a Super Spy 3: A Giant Problem!

Diary of a Super Spy 4: Space!

Diary of a Super Spy 5: Evil Attack!

Diary of a Super Spy 6: Daylight Robbery!

Made in the USA
Monee, IL
28 September 2020